Groundwood Books / House of Anansi Press
110 Spadina Avenue, Suite 801, Toronto, Ontario M5V 2K4
or c/o Publishers Group West
1700 Fourth Street, Berkeley, CA 94710

We acknowledge for their financial support of our publishing
program the Government of Canada through the Canada Book
Fund (CBF).

Library and Archives Canada Cataloguing in Publication

Schimel, Lawrence
Let's go see Papá! / Lawrence Schimel ; Alba Marina Rivera,
illustrator ; Elisa Amado, translator.

Translation of: ¡Vamos a ver a papá!
ISBN 978-1-55498-106-9

I. Rivera, Alba Marina   II. Amado, Elisa   III. Title.

PZ7.S355L3 2011   j813'.54   C2011-902087-4

The illustrations are in pencil, crayon, watercolor and acrylic,
combined with photocopies and transfers.
Printed and bound in China

Let's Go See Papá!

Lawrence Schimel   Pictures by Alba Marina Rivera

Translated by Elisa Amado

Groundwood Books / House of Anansi Press

Toronto   Berkeley

On Sundays I wake up early even though I don't have to go to school.

Papá's going to call us. He phones every Sunday because it's cheaper. Sunday is my favorite day.

I haven't seen my papá for one year, eight months and twenty-two days. I know because I've been counting since he went to the United States to work.

Before he left he gave me a blank notebook. Every day I write down what's happening in our house.

Papá couldn't come home for Christmas, so I sent him the notebook in the mail. He said he felt like I'd given him an extra year in his life — the year we'd lived through — besides the year he'd had on his own.

So I keep writing to him in a new notebook. I hope I can give it to him myself when he comes home.

Another thing I like about Sundays is that Mamá doesn't have to go to work.

We share a room here at my abuela's house.

I'm not alone when Mamá goes to work because Abuela and Kika are here, too.

When I go into the kitchen, Mamá and Abuela are already sitting at the table, drinking coffee.

Kika also loves the taste of coffee. Every morning my abuela pours a little on a piece of dry bread in her dish.

"Special breakfast for Kika," Abuela calls out.

I think coffee tastes really sour. I prefer a glass of milk.

"Good morning," I say.

They nod their heads, but we don't talk much because we are waiting for Papá's call.

Since Papá left we've waited a lot — waited for calls, waited for the money he sends us, waited for him to come home.

When Papá was here we always went out on Sundays to walk Kika and buy freshly baked bread. We'd walk hand in hand, and I'd try to take steps as big as his. We'd take Kika to the park. When we got there, I'd peer over the edge of the pond and count the goldfish. But then Kika would climb up and they'd hide.

FINALLY THE PHONE RINGS!

We all jump to our feet.

First Papá talks to Mamá, and then to Abuela, who is his mother. I wait for my turn.

"Papá, Iloveyou and Imissyou," I say, as fast as I can so it won't cost too much.

"I love you very much, too," he says. "Do you want to come and live with me here?"

I don't answer. I've been waiting to be together for so long. But I never imagined that I could go to where he is.

"Wh… wh… when?" I ask at last.

I feel confused after talking to Papá. I'm so happy that we are going to see him after such a long time! But I'm also a little bit scared. Everything will be really different. Will I make new friends?

Tonight, before going to bed, I take out the notebook where I write to Papá. But for the first time, I don't know what to put down.

On Monday, when I get to school, I tell my best friend, Rocío.

"I'm going to see my papá! But he's not coming here. We're going to go live with him in the United States."

"Wow, that's great!" says Rocío. "I'm jealous. Take me in your suitcase." And she winks at me.

"I'd like to," I answer, "because I don't know anyone there. I'm sure I'll never have another friend like you."

"Everything will be great. You'll see. And I'll write to you so I don't miss you too much," she says.

"I'll write to you, too," I answer.

Time goes by so slowly. Sometimes I even forget that we are going. But one day, Mamá brings home our airplane tickets, and everything suddenly speeds up.

"And Kika's ticket?" I ask.

Mamá looks at me for a moment without saying a word, and I know I'm not going to like her answer.

"Kika is staying here with Abuela," Mamá tells me.

My heart doesn't know how to be away from Kika. Every time I look at her and think that she's staying behind I feel like crying.

"I love you so much," I tell her and rub her tummy. "But you have to take care of Abuela so she doesn't feel alone, with her whole family living so far away."

Mamá explains that I can only take one suitcase.

I didn't know I had so much stuff. My dolls. My books. The pictures I painted at school. The postcards Papá sent. I can't take them all with me. They don't fit in the bag.

"Don't worry," Abuela says. "I'll keep the stuff that you can't take until you get back."

Abuela helps me choose. There are only a few things I really need. The most important thing is to be with Papá, I think.

Abuela seems to read my mind. "I wish I could go with you to see my son. But I'm too old to change my life. So you'll just have to take lots of kisses and hugs from me."

I cuddle up to my abuela.

"I'll miss you," I sob.

"Me, too," she says. And gives me lots of kisses. Then we go back to deciding what to pack until my suitcase is full.

The night before we leave, I'm so excited I can't sleep. I feel like my tummy is full of squirrels jumping around. Mamá doesn't sleep, either. I can tell by her breathing. I try to lie still so I don't bother her.

But I guess I slept a bit, because suddenly Abuela is calling me for breakfast.

I don't feel good. Abuela makes me drink a glass of milk, and after I drink it I do feel better.

Mamá goes over the list again so we don't forget anything.

"Where's Kika?" asks Abuela. "It's strange that she hasn't eaten her special breakfast."

I don't answer. I just sit and stare at my plate.

Abuela walks out of the kitchen calling Kika. There's a little sound from the bedroom, but it's hard to hear.

"What have you done with the dog?" asks Mamá and goes after Abuela.

I follow them both.

"It seems like she must be in here," says Abuela, "but I can't see her anywhere."

My suitcase moves.

"Kika!" Then Abuela scolds me. "How could you do this?"

"Where are your things?" asks Mamá. "We don't have time for these kinds of games."

Abuela and Mamá help me put my things back in the bag. It doesn't take long because now we know where everything goes. Kika tries to help, too.

We are being picked up to go to the airport in ten minutes.

"I'm taking Kika for a walk," I say, as I close the bag and run out of the house before they have time to say no.

I always talk to Kika when we go for a walk. I don't know what to say today. She jumps and runs like she always does.

I start to cry. I can't help it. Kika comes over to me and licks my face, as though she means to wipe away my tears. It makes me laugh. I lift up her ear and whisper, "Don't forget me."

Rocío and her father come around the corner. Kika runs to greet them.

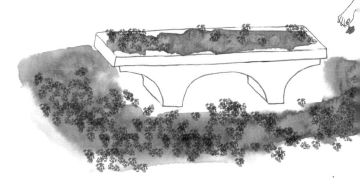

When everything is ready Abuela sits in front, next to Rocío's father. They chat about things and people they know, as though it were a completely normal day.

I'm behind, sitting between Mamá and Rocío. We don't say anything.

When we arrive at the airport, Rocío grabs my hand silently. She's the best friend in the whole world!

"We'll always be friends," I say, trying to smile.

We say goodbye over and over again, and I hug my abuela over and over, until they announce our flight and we have to go to the gate.

There's a lineup to get on the plane. I look down and Mamá puts her hand on my shoulder.

The flight attendant helps us find our seats. Mamá lets me sit by the window. I buckle my seat belt.

How tiny everything looks from up in the sky! Which house is Abuela's? What are she and Kika doing right now? Are they thinking about us? They must be, and Papá must be, too, right now.

I pull two notebooks out of my bag. One is the notebook I write in about everything we do for Papá. I open it, but I don't need to write in it anymore. In a few hours I'll be able to tell him everything myself. I feel happy to see so many white pages, because they mean lots of time when we won't be apart anymore.

I close Papá's notebook and I open the other one. It's new, with all blank pages. On the first page I write…

Dear Abuela,

I am in the plane, somewhere over the

ocean. It's scary to think about that.

But when I am writing to you, I can

almost forget that I'm up in the air,

crossing a huge sea...